This Walker book belongs to:

_____

_____

_____

Jonah

HANDSOME HARRY ★

WINKIE THE ONE-EYED BEAR

Pumpie

THE MAHARANA OF MEWAR 👉

Falooda

WOOLWORTH THE WOOLLEN OWL

Wee Scottie the Wind-up Dog

Augusta Marianna 🍀

Pip

MR JOLLYBOY

To Eva,
Jakob and Esmé

First published 2011 by Walker Books Ltd
87 Vauxhall Walk, London SE11 5HJ

This edition published 2012

2 4 6 8 10 9 7 5 3 1

Featuring characters from the collection of the V&A Museum of Childhood
www.museumofchildhood.org.uk

This book has been typeset in Berkeley Oldstyle

Printed in China

British Library Cataloguing in Publication Data:
a catalogue record for this book is available from the British Library

ISBN 978-1-4063-3852-2

www.walker.co.uk

WALKER BOOKS
AND SUBSIDIARIES

LONDON · BOSTON · SYDNEY · AUCKLAND

Christmas
at the
**TOY
MUSEUM**

by David Lucas

It was Christmas Eve, and all the
visitors to the Toy Museum were gone.
The lights went out, the doors were locked,
and Bunting and all the other toys
hurried to the big Christmas tree.

But there weren't any presents!
None at all.
Nothing for Christmas for any of them.

But Bunting had an idea.
A speech! He had to make a speech.

"Friends! Toys! Dolls! Puppets!"
he said. "Let us not be downhearted!
Why don't we all give each other
ourselves?"

It was an excellent speech,
and all the toys agreed it
was a wonderful idea.

And they all wrapped each
other in turn ...

until there was only Bunting left.

He climbed into a box
and shut his eyes tight.

All the toys stayed very still,
and tried not to rustle or fidget.

At the top of the tree, lived an angel.
She wasn't a toy angel, she was a REAL angel.

And she thought how kind the toys were
to give themselves to each other.

But she knew what would happen
on Christmas morning.

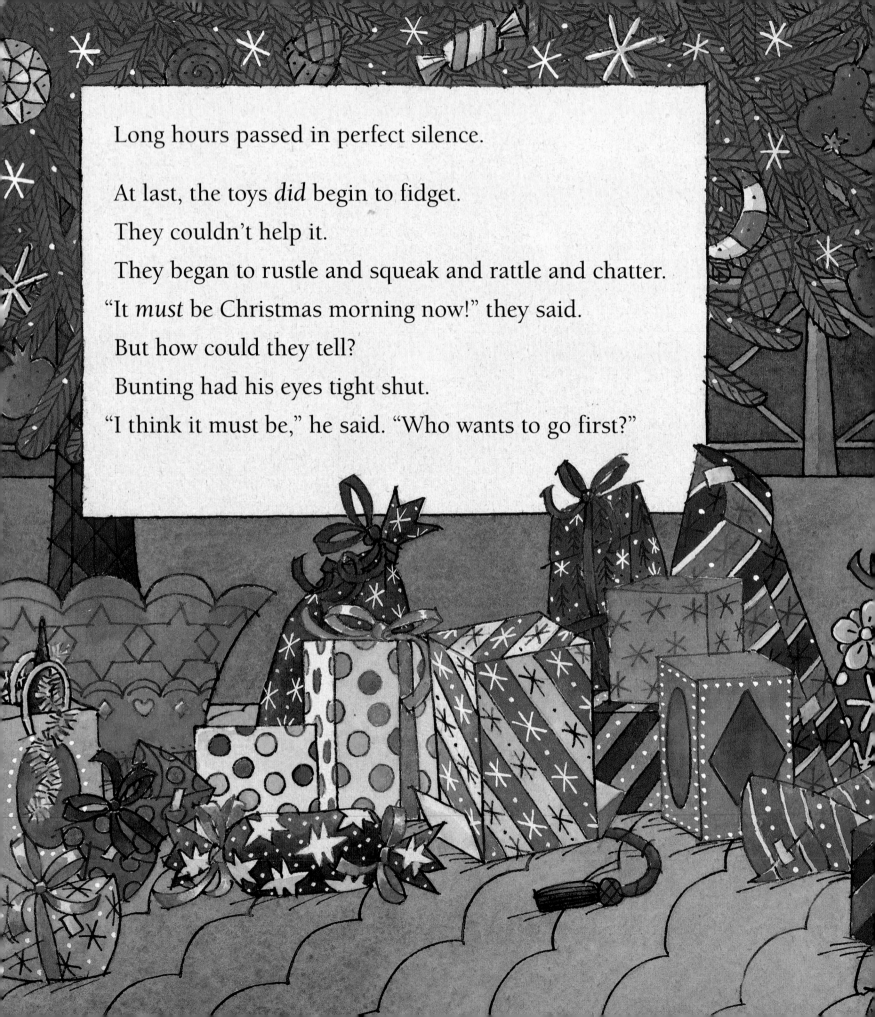

Long hours passed in perfect silence.

At last, the toys *did* begin to fidget.

They couldn't help it.

They began to rustle and squeak and rattle and chatter.

"It *must* be Christmas morning now!" they said.

But how could they tell?

Bunting had his eyes tight shut.

"I think it must be," he said. "Who wants to go first?"

"Me!" said Banger the Boxer Dog
and he sprang out of his wrapping.

And they all unwrapped
each other in turn ...

until last of all, Peg the Peg Doll
unwrapped Bunting.

Bunting looked at all the other toys.
There was no one for him to unwrap.
Bunting had *nothing* for Christmas.

High above, the angel smiled.
She had known this would happen, of course.

She spread her shining wings
and flew down from the top of the tree.

The toys gasped.

"Happy Christmas!" she said
and handed Bunting a golden box
tied with a golden ribbon.

And then the angel flew away.

"Open it! Open it!" said the toys, all together.
Bunting pulled on the ribbon.
Out jumped a little glowing star,
dancing in the air.

"I am a WISH," said the star.

"A wish?" said Bunting.
He knew just what to wish for.

"I wish that Christmas Day
could last for ever!" he said.

And it did.

HAPPY

Other books by David Lucas

ISBN 978-1-4063-3206-3

ISBN 978-1-4063-1958-3

Available from all good booksellers

www.walker.co.uk